Buttons the Runaway Puppy

Holly Webb

Illustrated by Sophy Williams

For Phoebe

www.hollywebbanimalstories.com

STRIPES PUBLISHING
An imprint of Little Tiger Press
1 The Coda Centre, 189 Munster Road,
London SW6 6AW

A paperback original
First published in Great Britain in 2009

ISBN: 978-1-84715-087-5

A CIP catalogue record for this book is available
from the British Library.

Printed and bound in the UK.

20 19 18 17 16 15 14 13 12

Buttons the Runaway Puppy

Other titles by Holly Webb

The Snow Bear

The Reindeer Girl

Animal Stories:

Lost in the Snow

Alfie all Alone

Lost in the Storm

Sam the Stolen Puppy

Max the Missing Puppy

Sky the Unwanted Kitten

Timmy in Trouble

Ginger the Stray Kitten

Harry the Homeless Puppy

Alone in the Night

Ellie the Homesick Puppy

Jess the Lonely Puppy

Misty the Abandoned Kitten

Oscar's Lonely Christmas

Lucy the Poorly Puppy

Smudge the Stolen Kitten

The Rescued Puppy

The Kitten Nobody Wanted

The Lost Puppy

The Frightened Kitten

The Secret Puppy

The Abandoned Puppy

The Missing Kitten

The Puppy Who Was Left Behind

The Kidnapped Kitten

My Naughty Little Puppy:

A Home for Rascal

New Tricks for Rascal

Playtime for Rascal

Rascal's Sleepover Fun

Rascal's Seaside Adventure

Rascal's Festive Fun

Rascal the Star

Rascal and the Wedding

Chapter One

"Wait for me!" Sophie called after her twin brothers. She was pedalling as fast as she could, but they were so much bigger than she was, and they'd had enormous new mountain bikes for their birthday last month. There was no way she could catch them up if they didn't slow down a bit. "Tom! Michael! Wait for me! Please!"

Tom and Michael circled round and hurtled back towards her, braking and pulling up in a cloud of dust.

"Come on, Sophie! You must be able to pedal a *bit* faster," Michael told her, laughing.

"Aw, now that's not fair, Mikey, she's only got little legs." Tom grinned at Sophie, and she scowled back.

"Can't we have a rest for a minute anyway?" she begged. "I want to watch the dogs, and this is the best bit of the common for that. I want to see if any of the ones I know are out for walks today."

"Yeah, I don't mind," Tom agreed.

Michael rolled his eyes. "Just for a minute. You're dog-mad, Sophie Martin!" he told her, grinning.

They wheeled their bikes out of the way of the path, and then slumped on a bench. All three of them stared out across the common, which was packed with dogs and their owners. This was definitely the best place for dog-watching: raised up on a little hill, they could see all the way around.

"Look, Sophie, there's that mad Red Setter you like." Michael pointed at a dog frisking about on one of the paths, its dark reddish coat gleaming in the sunlight.

Sophie giggled as she watched him running round and round in circles, and worrying at sticks. His owner was trying to get him to fetch a ball, but the big dog was having none of it.

Tom sighed. "If I had a dog, I'd train

it an awful lot better than that one. Poor thing doesn't know whether it's coming or going."

"I don't think it's very easy to train a dog," Sophie said.

"Of course it isn't," Tom agreed. "That's why there's so many badly behaved dogs around. People can't be bothered to train their dogs properly, and they just let them do whatever they want because it's easier than getting them to behave."

"OK then, if you could have any dog you want, what would you have?" Michael asked. "Mum and Dad keep saying that one day we can. Dad didn't say 'no' straight away last time I asked."

Tom whistled through his teeth. "Nothing small and yappy. A dog you could take on proper walks. Maybe a Dalmatian."

"Mmm, I could go for a Dalmatian. Or a Golden Retriever," Michael mused. "Wouldn't it be great to get a dog now, just before the summer holidays? We'd have all summer to go for really long walks."

Tom nodded. "Don't get your hopes up. What would you have, Sophie?"

Sophie was staring back down the path that they'd come up. "I'd have a Labrador. But a chocolate one, like Buttons. I *think* that's her coming up the path now. Oh dear…"

"What's she done this time?" Tom asked.

Sophie put her hand over her mouth to stifle her giggles, as the chocolate-brown Labrador puppy danced around her owner, tangling him in her lead.

"Whoops," Tom muttered, and Michael bobbed up from the bench to see what was going on.

"Ow, that must've hurt. Do you think we should go and help?"

Buttons was standing on the path, looking down at her owner in confusion.

What on earth are you doing down there?
she seemed to be saying. Her owner
unwrapped her lead from his ankles
grimly, and started to heave himself up
out of the bramble bush.

Sophie looked at Tom and Michael.
"We probably should, but Buttons's
owner is so grumpy, he might shout
at us."

"He's called Mr Jenkins," Tom told her. "I heard one of his neighbours talking to him when we walked past his house the other day."

Michael nodded. "I think Sophie's right, he's probably hoping no one saw. We'd better be looking the other way when he comes past."

All three children stared innocently over the common towards the lake, pretending not to have seen Buttons trip up Mr Jenkins.

"Good morning!" Michael called politely, as the old man walked by, trying to hold Buttons back to heel. Mr Jenkins lived on the next road across from the Martins, with his garden backing on to theirs, so they saw him quite often. Their mum always said hello when she passed him.

"Hmmph," Mr Jenkins grunted, and stomped on past.

"You see! So grumpy!" Sophie whispered, as he disappeared down the path.

"Yes, but I'd be grumpy too, if I'd just fallen in a bramble bush," Tom pointed out.

Buttons appreciated them saying hello, anyway. She looked back and barked in a friendly way as Mr Jenkins hurried her along. She liked those children. They always smiled when they saw her, and the girl had once asked politely to stroke her. Mr Jenkins had let her, and she'd said how beautiful Buttons was and scratched behind her ears as well.

"Come on, Buttons," Mr Jenkins grumbled, and Buttons sighed. He was cross with her again. She hadn't *meant* to trip him up. There were so many good smells on the common, and she couldn't help it if they were on different sides of the path. She'd had to go and investigate them all, and the silly lead had got itself tangled in his legs. It just showed that leads were not a good idea. She much preferred to run along without one. Especially if there were squirrels.

They were coming to the part of the common with the trees now, and there was bound to be a squirrel. Buttons looked up and barked hopefully.

"No, I'm not letting you off your

lead, silly dog," Mr Jenkins told her, but he patted her lovingly on the head at the same time, and she knew he wasn't cross any more. "No, because you'll be in the next county before I catch up with you. I'm sorry, Buttons girl, we need to head home. My legs aren't what they used to be, especially when I've been dragged through a bramble bush. Come on, home now."

Buttons whined sadly. She understood some words, and *home* was one of them. Not home already? It felt like it hadn't been a very long walk at all. She wanted lots of walks – in fact a whole day of walks, with a few quick sleeps and a couple of big meals in between, would be perfect.

"Look, Mum, Buttons is in her garden again." Sophie nudged her mother's arm as they walked past Mr Jenkins's house. The summer holidays had started, and it was so hot that they were going to cool off at the pool. "She keeps scrabbling at the fence like she wants to get out. She was doing that yesterday, when I went past on my way to say goodbye to Rachel. I heard her barking loads when I was out in the garden, too."

Mum stopped and looked thoughtfully over the fence at Buttons. "Have you seen Mr Jenkins about recently?" she asked Sophie. "I haven't for a while, and I do usually meet him in the shops every so often."

Sophie shook her head. "Not since that day in the park a couple of weeks ago, when Buttons tripped him up. I definitely haven't seen him since school finished, and that's a whole week."

She sighed. Only one week of the summer holidays gone. She ought to be looking forward to another five weeks off school, but yesterday her best friend Rachel had gone off to Ireland to stay with her family for the whole holiday. Sophie couldn't imagine what she was going to do all summer, without Rachel's house to hang out at. She was sick of Michael and Tom already. Not only were they her big brothers, so they thought they could always boss her around, but they were each other's best friends. They didn't want their little sister tagging along the whole time. She and Rachel had promised to keep in touch by email and send each other lots of fun postcards and things. But it wasn't the same as having your best friend living just round the corner.

Buttons looked up at Sophie and barked hopefully. *Walk? Please?* she begged. She recognized Sophie, who often spoke to her when she went past. Buttons could sometimes hear her in the garden, too. Sophie had a sweet voice and always sounded friendly.

"Poor Buttons, she looks really sad," Sophie said, wishing she could stroke her. She knew Buttons was friendly, but Mum had made her promise not to stroke dogs without asking the owner first.

"Thinking about it, I did see Mr Jenkins in the supermarket last week, and he was walking with a stick," Mum said slowly. "I wonder if he hasn't been able to take Buttons for walks, and that's why she's scratching like that. She wants to get out."

"Sorry, Buttons, we're going swimming, or else we'd love to take you for a walk. Oh, look, I'm sure she knows what we're saying, her ears just drooped, and she isn't wagging her tail any more," Sophie said as she waved goodbye.

Buttons stared after them with big, sad brown eyes. She hadn't been on a proper walk in a long time. Mr Jenkins was very good about letting her in and out of the house whenever she wanted, but he just didn't seem to want to walk her right now. The garden was quite big — it went all round the house from front to back — but it wasn't the same as walks. Buttons whined sadly, and scratched at the fence again. She thought she might be able to go for a walk by herself, if she could only get over this fence. Or under it, perhaps.

"Buttons! Buttons!" She could hear Mr Jenkins calling, and her ears pricked up immediately. Maybe he was feeling better, and he wanted to go for a walk after all. She shot round to the back door, which Mr Jenkins was holding open for her.

"There you are! You've been out a while, Buttons." Mr Jenkins stooped down to pat her, holding tight to his stick.

Buttons looked up at him hopefully, and then looked over at her lead, which was hanging on a hook above Mr Jenkins's wellies. She gave an excited little bark, and wagged her tail so fast it blurred.

"Oh, Buttons, I wish we could. I wish we could, poor little girl. Soon, I promise."

Buttons's tail sagged, and she trailed slowly into the living room to curl up on her cushion next to Mr Jenkins's chair. He sat down beside her, and stroked her head lovingly. Buttons licked his hand. She adored Mr Jenkins, even though he couldn't always take her for walks.

Chapter Two

"If you're going along the canal path, you have to be really careful," Mum warned them. "Especially you, Sophie. No going close to the edge, promise?"

"I'm not a baby, Mum! I'm sensible!" Sophie complained. "OK, I promise to be careful."

"All right then. Tom and Michael, you'll keep an eye on her, won't you?

Don't leave her behind."

Sophie's older brothers nodded, eager to get out on their ride, even if it did mean taking Sophie, too.

It was a gorgeous, sunny Saturday afternoon, and Mum and Dad were repainting the kitchen, so it was definitely a good time to be out of the house. The canal path was the Martin family's other favourite place to go on walks and bike rides. They were lucky that it wasn't far from where they lived.

Despite what they'd said to Mum, Michael and Tom couldn't resist speeding off ahead. Every so often one of them would double back to check Sophie was OK, and she was – she quite liked riding along on her own anyway. It meant she could stop and talk to the ginger cat sitting on the fence – he let her stroke him today – and admire the butterflies on a lilac tree that grew on the corner just as she came out on to the canal bank. She could do all these things without the boys telling her to hurry up all the time.

Sophie pedalled along, keeping away from the edge like Mum had told her to. The canal was beautiful, especially with the sun sparkling on it like it was today, but beneath the glitter the water was deep and dark. She rounded the bend, expecting to see Tom and Michael coming back to check on her, but instead she saw a familiar-looking dog.

Buttons!

The pretty little Labrador was sniffing about at the water's edge. Sophie cycled closer, smiling at Buttons's big chocolate paws, and her floppy puppy ears.

Sophie looked around for Mr Jenkins, but she couldn't see him anywhere, and she had a horrible feeling that Buttons had run off. She wasn't old enough or sensible enough to be off the lead – and she wasn't, it was trailing in the mud. Buttons must've pulled it out of Mr Jenkins's hand.

Buttons hadn't noticed Sophie. She was watching a stick that was floating down the canal, and wondering whether she could reach it, if she just leaned over a little. It looked like such a good one – big and long and really muddy – and it was ever so close. She leaned out over the water. If she could just get the end of it in her teeth… But it was still a bit too far away. She tried again, reaching a little further out.

"Buttons! Don't!" Sophie called. "You'll fall!"

Surprised by Sophie's shout, Buttons stepped back quickly. But the edge of the canal bank was muddy and slippery, and her paws skidded. Panicking, she tried to scramble back up the bank, but she was sliding further in, and she couldn't stop herself.

Sophie flung down her bike, and raced to grab Buttons's lead. She caught it just as both of the puppy's front paws slid into the water. Sophie pulled hard on the lead, leaning right back – Buttons might only be little, but she was heavy. Just for a moment, Sophie wondered if Buttons might accidentally pull her into the water, too, but she finally hauled Buttons back on to the bank.

She hugged the shivering puppy tightly. "It's all right, Buttons. Oh dear, your paws are all wet. It's OK, don't worry," Sophie murmured soothingly, trying to calm her down. Buttons buried her nose in Sophie's T-shirt, breathing in her comforting smell. Sophie had saved her!

"Buttons! Buttons!" Mr Jenkins was hurrying up, walking as fast as he could with his stick. "What happened, did she fall in?" he asked worriedly. "I saw you pulling her lead, are you all right? Is she all right?"

He leaned down slowly to stroke Buttons, and she pressed herself against his legs, making frightened little whimpering noises. "Oh, Buttons, you silly girl, what have you been doing?"

He looked up and smiled apologetically at Sophie. "She pulled her lead out of my hand and raced off. It's the first time we've been for a walk in a while. Buttons is a bit overexcited to be out again."

Sophie smiled back at him, though her heart was still thumping. It had been a scary moment. "She didn't go right in. She was just starting to slip, but I grabbed her lead before she did more than get her paws wet."

"Sophie! Are you OK?" Tom and Michael had come riding up, and they looked worried. The little sister they were supposed to be looking after was sitting on the canal bank with a wet dog, her bike flung down on the grass.

"Were you messing about by the

water? Mum told you to stay away from the edge!" Tom shouted.

"Of course I wasn't!" Sophie said indignantly.

Mr Jenkins looked up at the boys. "Your sister stopped Buttons falling in. She's a star. Ooof." He slowly straightened up. "I think we were a bit ambitious with this walk, Buttons. Best leave it a couple of days more."

"Would you like me to walk Buttons home for you?" Sophie asked.

Mr Jenkins smiled at her. "It's very kind of you to offer, but you weren't going home yet, were you? I don't want to take you out of your way."

"That's all right. Isn't it?" Sophie asked Tom and Michael. "Mum wouldn't mind if I went back, would she?"

The boys exchanged glances. "We'll come too," said Tom. "That way we can wheel your bike while you're walking Buttons."

"Oh! I'd forgotten my bike," Sophie admitted. "I was too excited about getting to walk such a gorgeous puppy."

"She is lovely, isn't she?" Mr Jenkins agreed, as they all started to walk home slowly. "Bit of a handful at the moment though. She's got so much energy."

Buttons was darting here and there, sniffing excitedly at the scents of other dogs and people. Sophie laughed as she followed her, but she could see that such a bouncy little dog would be hard work for Mr Jenkins.

"I really need to take her to some dog-training classes, but we just haven't been able to get out much recently. Soon though," Mr Jenkins added, as he watched Buttons racing about.

"Where did you get her from?" Sophie asked, wishing she could have a beautiful chocolate-coloured dog like Buttons.

"She came from a breeder who lives over on the other side of town. I got my last two dogs from him as well, but they were golden Labradors. Buttons is the first chocolate one I've had."

"Buttons is such a brilliant name for a chocolate Labrador," Sophie told him, giggling.

"Ah, that wasn't me. It was my granddaughter Phoebe's idea. She thought it was really funny."

"Does she live round here?" Sophie asked. "I don't know anyone called Phoebe at school."

"No." Mr Jenkins shook his head, sadly. "My son had to move with work earlier in the year. They live in Scotland now. I try and get up to see them, but I do miss her."

Sophie nodded. "That's sad. My grandad lives in France; we don't see him much either. And my nan and my other grandad live in London, ages away. We phone them lots, but it isn't the same as seeing them, is it?"

Mr Jenkins sighed. "Not at all. Phoebe hasn't even seen Buttons yet; I got her six weeks ago. I've sent some photos."

Buttons was enjoying following all

the delicious smells, and with Sophie holding her lead, she could go as fast as she liked. She was sure that there had been a mouse along here recently. It had gone this way, stopped here, then doubled back over here – oh! She was almost at the water's edge. She stepped back, whining. She loved to look at the water, but she didn't want to be in it.

Buttons looked up gratefully at Sophie, who was gripping her lead tightly. She was very glad that Sophie had been there to pull her out before. She knew she shouldn't have run off from Mr Jenkins like that, but they'd been going so slowly. Still she wouldn't do it again, it was far too dangerous. She wouldn't run away ever again...

Chapter Three

Sophie and the boys said goodbye to Mr Jenkins at the door. The old man was very grateful, and told Sophie that she was quick-thinking and helpful, and she reminded him of his granddaughter.

"That's all right," Sophie said, blushing, as she took her bike back from Tom. "I'm glad I was there to catch her."

Sophie watched as Mr Jenkins let himself and Buttons into the house, then she and the boys pedalled home excitedly.

Luckily Mum and Dad were having a break from painting, so they were able to listen to Sophie when she dashed in, full of her news.

"Well done, Sophie." Her dad smiled, but then he looked worried. "I hope you were careful, though. A big dog like a Labrador could've easily pulled you in, too."

"Oh no, Dad, Buttons is only little – she's just a puppy," Sophie explained. Then she noticed that Michael and Tom were making faces at her behind Dad's back and added, "And Tom and Mike were only a bit ahead of me; they'd have pulled me out if I *had* fallen in."

Her mum shuddered. "Well, thank goodness you didn't."

"I think Soph deserves an ice cream for being clever," her dad put in. "I could do with one too, after all that painting. Want to run down to the shop?"

"Oooh, yes!" And Sophie gave him a hug, carefully minding the painty bits.

When they were all sitting round in the garden eating their ice creams, Sophie said thoughtfully, "Mum, do you think Mr Jenkins would like me to walk Buttons for him while his leg's bad? He said he'd have to take it easy for a couple more days, but I think a dog like Buttons needs proper walks *every* day."

Mum and Dad exchanged glances,

and Mum sighed. "You're right, Sophie. She would need lots of walks, a young energetic dog like that. Probably Mr Jenkins could do with some help. But it's tricky. We don't want to make him feel like we're interfering, or that we think he can't cope. If he asked, it would be different…"

"I bet he won't ask," Tom said, through a mouthful of ice cream. "He's not that sort of person."

"Well, if I see him, I'll try and sound him out," Mum suggested. "OK? A compromise."

Sophie nodded reluctantly. Poor Buttons. It looked like she was going to be stuck in the garden again for a while.

Buttons followed Mr Jenkins into the house a little sadly. It had been fun walking with Sophie. Buttons tried hard not to pull on her lead with Mr Jenkins; she could tell it was hard for him to walk. She forgot sometimes, that was all. It was hard to remember to be careful when she smelled something yummy, or saw something she just had to chase. With Sophie, she had felt it was all right to be her bouncy puppy self and Buttons hoped she would see her again soon. Maybe Mr Jenkins would take her on a walk tomorrow.

But he didn't. On Monday morning, Buttons hopefully brought him her lead, just in case, but he was sitting in his chair, recovering from the effort of getting down the stairs.

"I'm sorry, Buttons. Not today."
He sighed as he took her lead and
heaved himself up. "You go and have a
run round the garden, there's a good
girl. And I'll put your food down for
you in a minute."

Buttons could feel him watching her
as she skittered off down the garden.
He looked anxious, and she wondered
what was wrong. He was holding her
lead still, and looking at it sadly.

Buttons looked around the garden and gave a little whine. She would much prefer a walk, but the garden was better than nothing. She was sniffing thoughtfully through the flower bed by the fence, when she came across a little hole under a bush. It was just large enough to get her nose into, but the loose dirt made her back out quickly, sneezing and shaking her muzzle.

Once she'd stopped pawing at her nose, Buttons sat and looked at the hole, with her head on one side. It was only a small hole. But she was quite sure it could be bigger. If there was a hole under the fence, she could go off for a walk by herself. Without even her lead! Buttons crouched down, and started to scrape at the earth with one paw...

The hole took a while to dig, but no one noticed what Buttons was doing because of the bush. It was a perfect cover.

Late the next afternoon, Buttons wriggled and squirmed her way out under the fence, and stood in the street, looking round in delight. She could explore! She could go wherever she wanted! She sniffed the air eagerly. Which way should she go first? The most delicious smells wafted past her and she pattered off down the street, looking around curiously.

On a wall two doors down from Mr Jenkins's house, a black cat was snoozing in the sun, its tail dangling invitingly down the side of the wall. Buttons trotted up to it and barked. She'd been shut up in the garden for ages and she wanted to run. It would be even better if she could chase something! She didn't know that chasing cats wasn't allowed – there was just something about the cat that made her want to bark at it...

The cat woke up with a start, and mewed frantically, its tail puffing out and all the fur standing up along its back.

Buttons stood at the bottom of the wall, barking excitedly, and the cat hissed and spat.

"Go away! Bad dog!" A woman was hurrying down the garden path, waving a trowel crossly.

Buttons didn't know what she'd done wrong, but she knew what bad dog meant. She slunk away with her tail between her legs, just in time to see Mr Jenkins standing at his gate, looking around for her worriedly.

"Is this your dog?" the cat's owner demanded. "She's been terrorizing my poor Felix. You should keep her shut up properly!"

"I'm sorry." Mr Jenkins limped out and caught Buttons by the collar. "I don't know how she got out. Has she hurt the cat?"

"Well, no," the lady admitted. "But he's terrified!" And she stomped back round the side of her house, carrying Felix and muttering about badly-behaved dogs.

"Oh, Buttons." Mr Jenkins sighed.

Buttons looked up at him apologetically, giving her tail a hopeful little wag. She hadn't been that naughty, had she?

Mr Jenkins didn't know about the hole Buttons had dug under the fence. He thought that the postman must have let her out, or the boy delivering the local paper. He put a notice on the gate reminding people to shut it carefully, and kept Buttons in for the rest of the day.

The next day, Sophie went out to send a postcard to Rachel. The postbox was in the next street to hers – the street where Mr Jenkins and

Buttons lived. Sophie was hoping she might see Buttons on the way; she was sure she'd heard her barking from her garden. Mr Jenkins might be in the garden, too – Mum hadn't had a chance to ask him about Sophie walking Buttons, and Sophie was tempted to ask him herself.

On her way back from sending her postcard, Sophie was just coming round the corner towards Mr Jenkins's house, when she heard a scuffling noise, loud barking and someone shouting.

Sophie hurried round the corner. Buttons was out! The little brown dog was standing with her front paws on the wall, barking at a black cat who was perched on the top, hissing and trying to claw at Buttons's nose.

"Oh, Buttons, no!" Sophie cried, running over. "You mustn't chase cats!"

The black cat jumped from the wall into the safety of a tree. Buttons barked one last flurry of barks, then looked guiltily at Sophie. She'd been told off about this yesterday, but she'd forgotten. Cats were just so tempting!

"Do you know this dog? Can you grab her collar, please?" A woman was hurrying up the garden path. "I need to take her back to her owner. This is the third time she's chased my cat; she was out this morning as well."

Sophie caught hold of Buttons's collar, and patted her gently to try and calm her down. Buttons wriggled, so Sophie picked her up instead, and the puppy snuggled gratefully into her arms.

"Be careful!" the cat's owner said anxiously. "She's snappy! Vicious little thing."

Sophie looked at the woman in surprise. Buttons? Sophie was sure she wasn't vicious, just a bit naughty.

The woman came out of her garden, looking worriedly up at her cat, and opened Mr Jenkins's gate. "Would you be able to take her back? She seems to behave for you. I really need to talk to Mr Jenkins, this is getting silly."

Sophie followed her, almost wishing she hadn't gone out to send her postcard. She was glad she'd been able to catch Buttons – the little dog could have been hurt if she'd run into the road – but she didn't want to be in the middle of an argument between Mr Jenkins and his neighbour.

Mr Jenkins answered the door, and he looked horrified when he saw them. "Mrs Lane! Sophie! Oh, Buttons, not again..."

"Again," Mrs Lane said grimly. "The third time. You promised me this morning you wouldn't let her out!"

"I really am sorry, Mrs Lane. I've

got someone coming to block up the hole under the fence later on, and I've kept Buttons shut in ever since I found it. She must've climbed out of the window." He gestured at an open window, and Sophie noticed that the flowers underneath looked rather squashed.

"If this happens again, I'll have to report you to the council," Mrs Lane said crossly. Then she sighed. "I'm sorry, I don't mean to be rude. But you're just not keeping her properly under control. She's a little terror!"

Mr Jenkins frowned. "I can only apologize, and promise you that it won't happen again." He sighed and leaned wearily against the door frame.

"Please make sure that it doesn't."

Mrs Lane looked at him and her voice softened. "Are you all right, Mr Jenkins? Would you like me to call your doctor? You really don't look very well."

Mr Jenkins stood up very straight. "I'm perfectly fine, thank you," he said coldly. "Sophie, could you pass Buttons to me, please?"

Sophie handed Buttons over a little reluctantly. Mrs Lane was right – he didn't look well, and she was worried Buttons was too heavy for him to carry. But she didn't dare say so. "Bye, Mr Jenkins; bye, Buttons," she whispered.

Mrs Lane stalked back down the path, and Sophie followed her, looking back to see Mr Jenkins closing the window to a tiny crack, and Buttons standing next to him now, with her paws on the window sill – Sophie guessed the puppy was standing on a chair – staring sadly after her. "See you soon, Buttons!" she whispered. Maybe next time she'd ask about being allowed to walk her.

That night, Sophie sat curled up in bed, staring out of her window. Her room was at the back of the house, and she could see the big tree in Mr Jenkins's garden and his house beyond. Buttons was in there. At least, Sophie hoped she was. She'd been lying in bed, thinking about how she'd go and see Mr Jenkins tomorrow and ask him about walking Buttons, but then she'd had an awful thought.

What if the little dog had already got out again? Sophie had a horrible feeling that if Buttons could dig one hole under the fence, then it wouldn't be long before she'd make another one. And this time she'd be in *real* trouble.

I should have been brave enough to ask Mr Jenkins about walking her, she thought miserably, one tear trickling slowly down her cheek. If Buttons didn't get walked, she'd keep trying to go out by herself. That grumpy lady had said she'd call the council if Buttons chased her cat again.

"Sophie! Why are you still awake? It's really late." Her mum was looking round the door. "Oh, Sophie, what's wrong?" She came in and sat on the end of the bed. "You're crying!"

"Mum, what would happen to a dog if somebody called the council about her?" Sophie asked worriedly.

Her mum put an arm round her shoulders. "I – I don't know, Sophie. Is this about Buttons?" Sophie had told her what had happened earlier on.

"Mrs Lane said she'd call the council. They'd take Buttons away from Mr Jenkins, Mum, I know they would. She'd get put in the dogs' home."

Her mum sighed. "I know it's hard to accept, but that might not be a bad thing…"

"Mum!" Sophie looked shocked.

"You've been saying that Mr Jenkins can't walk Buttons enough, Sophie. She's only going to get bigger, and stronger. She's not an old man's dog. She's such a sweet little thing, she'd probably be adopted by a lovely family."

"But she loves Mr Jenkins!" Sophie

told her anxiously. "You can see from the way she looks at him. And he's really lonely, with all his family so far away. He needs her, Mum." She didn't add that if Buttons got a new home, she'd never see her again – it seemed really selfish. But she couldn't help *thinking* it.

Sophie's mum nodded sadly. "I know. I'm sorry, Sophie. I just don't think there's a right answer to all of this." She stood up, and pulled Sophie's bedcover straight. "Try and go to sleep, OK?"

Sophie nodded. But after her mum had gone, she went back to looking out of the window, and thinking about poor Buttons, just across the garden. "Be good, Buttons!" she murmured, as she finally lay down to sleep.

Chapter Four

Buttons had just finished her breakfast, and she was playing with one of the new chew toys Mr Jenkins had got to keep her entertained, when she heard a terrible, sliding crash. She dashed into the hallway, where the noise seemed to have come from.

Mr Jenkins was lying in a crumpled heap at the bottom of the stairs.

Buttons howled in shock and fright. Her owner wasn't moving. It looked as though he'd tripped over his stick on the way down the stairs. Miserably, she waited for him to get up.

He didn't.

After waiting for a few minutes, staring worriedly at his closed eyes and pale face, Buttons nosed him gently. Was he asleep?

Mr Jenkins groaned, and Buttons jumped back in surprise. That wasn't a good noise.

"Buttons..." he murmured. "Good girl. I'll get up in a minute. Oh..." But as he tried to move, Mr Jenkins collapsed back again, groaning. "No, I can't." He was silent for a moment, breathing fast. "Buttons, go fetch help.

Go on…" His voice died away, and his eyes closed again, as Buttons watched him anxiously.

He didn't stir, even when Buttons licked his face, very gently.

Buttons whined. He'd said to fetch help, but she wasn't sure what he meant. Sophie! She would get Sophie. Buttons was sure she would know what to do.

Buttons backed away from Mr Jenkins slowly, and looked at the front door. It was closed. She trotted down the hallway and into the kitchen. The back door was shut, too. She nudged it hopefully. Mr Jenkins had let her out first thing – perhaps he hadn't quite closed it properly? But it was shut fast, and pawing at it did nothing.

She walked back up the hallway. Mr Jenkins hadn't moved. People weren't meant to be that still. She had to get out and find Sophie! Buttons stood by the door and barked as loudly as she could, hoping that someone would come and open it for her, but no one did.

She stared at the door for a minute, then went into the living room. Buttons eyed the window.

She knew she wasn't supposed to do this. Mr Jenkins had said no, very crossly and that she must never do it again.

But what else was she supposed to do? No one had come when she called. The doors were all shut. It was the only way out, and Mr Jenkins needed help.

Buttons clambered on to the armchair and up on to the backrest, so that her front paws were on the window sill. Then she stuck her nose through the window. It was only open a crack. Mr Jenkins liked fresh air, and he always had the windows open, but he had almost shut this one because of the time she'd climbed out of the window before. But when she pushed with her nose the window opened just a crack more.

Now she could get her ears through – although it was a squeeze and it hurt. Buttons wriggled her shoulders as if she were shaking water out of her fur, and scrabbled and scrambled and finally tumbled out of the window, landing clumsily in the flower bed underneath.

She wasn't excited by the idea of a trip, like she'd been yesterday. Now she wanted to be curled up next to Mr Jenkins's armchair, his hand stroking her ears, watching one of those delicious food programmes on the television.

Buttons headed for her little hole under the fence, but when she wriggled under the bush, it wasn't there! She lay there staring at the fence, whimpering in confusion. Brand-new boards had been nailed across the bottom, and her hole had been completely blocked up. She'd gone through all that trouble to get into the garden, and now she couldn't get out.

Suddenly Buttons's ears pricked up. She could hear Sophie! Sophie was in her garden on the other side of the back fence. She wriggled out from under the bush, barking loudly as she ran to the other end of the garden.

"Hi, Buttons!" Sophie called back, laughing, and Buttons barked louder. Sophie didn't understand! She thought Buttons was just barking to be friendly, like she sometimes did. She would have to get out of the garden and go and get Sophie. She gave a few more loud barks, then scampered back to look at the gate.

She had tried to open it before, and it hadn't worked, but she had been smaller then. She would try again. She scratched at it, but nothing much happened. It shook a little, but that was all. Buttons took a few steps back and looked up. That silvery part sticking out at the top was what made it open, she was sure. It clicked and rattled when people came in. If she could pull it across, the gate would open. And she thought she was tall enough now, if she really stretched.

Luckily for Buttons, the bolt was old and loose, but not rusty, and when she dragged at it with her strong, young teeth, it slid back easily enough. The gate opened, and Buttons sat in front of it, looking out at the street in amazement. She had done it!

Now all she had to do was find Sophie.

Buttons trotted out into the street. Then she stared back at the house, one last time, hoping the front door would open, and Mr Jenkins would come out, saying he was all right now. She wouldn't even mind if he told her off for opening the gate.

But the door stayed firmly shut. Buttons looked up and down the road. She needed to find Sophie's house. Maybe she could sniff her out.

"Naughty dog!" someone shouted, and Buttons raced off. She knew that voice – the angry lady with the cat. She wanted Buttons to come back, but Buttons wasn't going to let anyone stop her now.

Buttons sped round the corner, looking back over her shoulder anxiously. No one was following. Good. She looked at the houses on either side of the road, and her tail drooped. How was she supposed to know which house was Sophie's? She was sure it had to be along here somewhere – she could feel that she'd gone in the right direction. But working out exactly which house lined up with hers was beyond her.

Perhaps she could call Sophie? She barked hopefully, then louder and louder again. Nothing happened.

Buttons sat down in the middle of the pavement and howled. She would never find Sophie.

"Buttons!"

Sophie came running along the pavement towards her, followed by Tom and Michael. "I told you I heard her barking. There *is* something wrong, I know there is. Oh no, I hope she hasn't been chasing that cat."

Buttons ran up to them, wagging her tail gratefully. She'd almost given up.

"We'd better take her back," Tom said. "Grab her collar, Sophie, we don't want her to run into the road."

But when Sophie tried to catch hold of Buttons, she backed off.

"What's the matter, Buttons?" Sophie asked, feeling confused.

"She looks upset," Michael commented. "She isn't wagging her tail any more. She isn't hurt, is she?"

Sophie crouched down and tried to

call the puppy over. "Here, Buttons, come on. Good girl." But Buttons whimpered, and looked anxiously down the street.

Sophie frowned. "I think she wants us to follow her. Come on! Show me, good dog, Buttons." And Sophie grabbed Tom and Michael by the hand and dragged them after her.

Buttons ran along in front of them, turning every few steps to check they were following.

"I hope something hasn't happened to Mr Jenkins," Michael muttered.

"What do you mean?" Sophie asked in an anxious voice.

"I can't think why else she'd be so desperate for us to follow her," Michael explained reluctantly.

"Let's go faster," said Sophie, speeding up. "He looked awful when I took Buttons back yesterday."

They reached the house, panting, and Buttons pushed open the gate. Then she ran to the door, and paced back and forth between the door and the open window, whining. *Hurry, hurry!* she tried to tell them. *Let me in! You have to help him!*

Sophie rang the bell, but she didn't really expect anyone to answer it.

Buttons barked, sounding more and more desperate, and Tom pulled out his mobile. "Do you think we should call the police?" he asked. "Or try the neighbours?"

"Shhhh!" Sophie said suddenly. "Listen. I can hear something."

Faintly, from inside the house, she could hear a voice. Even Buttons stopped barking. She listened too, and she heard Mr Jenkins saying, "Help! Buttons, are you there? Sophie, is that you?"

"He's calling for help!" Sophie gasped. She scrabbled at the door handle, her fingers slipping. She was sure it hadn't been locked when she'd brought Buttons back before.

"Not the police, an ambulance," Tom muttered, when Sophie had got the door open and he saw Mr Jenkins lying at the foot of the stairs. "Don't move him!" he called to Sophie, who was kneeling beside the old man, her hand on Buttons's collar.

"I won't," Sophie said. "Mr Jenkins, Buttons found us. Did you send her to fetch us? She's so clever, she made us follow her."

Mr Jenkins looked up at her, smiling a little. "I knew she'd get help," he whispered. "Good dog, Buttons."

And Buttons licked his cheek, very, very gently.

Chapter Five

By the time the ambulance arrived, Mr Jenkins was looking very slightly better. There was a touch of colour in his cheeks. Buttons sat next to him, watching over him and every so often licking his hand.

The ambulance men were very impressed that Buttons had fetched Sophie, Tom and Michael.

They stroked her, and said how clever she was.

Mr Jenkins smiled, and then his face fell. "Buttons! What's going to happen to her? There's no one to take her!"

"We can arrange for her to go to the shelter for you, for a while," one of the ambulance men suggested gently.

"No, no, she'd hate that..." Mr Jenkins stared at Buttons worriedly.

Buttons whimpered, not knowing what was wrong.

"Careful now," the ambulance man warned, trying to soothe the old man. "Don't upset yourself."

"Tom, can't you ring Mum and Dad?" Sophie begged. "We could take Buttons; I'm sure they'd say 'yes' if we explained what had happened."

Mr Jenkins nodded gratefully. "That would be wonderful."

Tom grabbed his phone out of his pocket. Sophie watched nervously as he explained everything to Mum. "She said to bring her back with us," he said at last, smiling. "She wasn't sure, but she said OK."

"Go with Sophie, Buttons," Mr Jenkins whispered, as the ambulance men carried his stretcher away down the path. "There's a good girl."

The ambulance sped away with its blue lights flashing, and Buttons whimpered as she stared after it, watching until it disappeared round the corner. Then she looked up trustingly at Sophie. Mr Jenkins had said to go with her, so she would.

Just at that moment, Mrs Lane, Mr Jenkins's neighbour, came hurrying down the street. She had seen the ambulance, and she looked worried.

"Oh my goodness, was that Mr Jenkins?" she asked the children, and when they nodded, she dropped her shopping bag, and her face went pale. "I knew I should have made him see a doctor," she murmured. "But he was so stubborn. Oh! The dog! What on earth are we going to do with her?"

"We're taking her home with us," Sophie said firmly.

Mrs Lane looked surprised, but rather relieved. "I can't possibly take her, you know. She chases Felix," she said very firmly.

Tom and Michael carried Buttons's things out of the house, and Sophie clipped on her lead. Mr Jenkins had said to take everything they needed, and given them his door key to lock up afterwards.

"Don't let her get out," Mrs Lane advised as she stood watching.

Sophie, Tom and Michael smiled politely, and didn't say anything, but as soon as they were round the corner – the boys laden down with baskets and bowls and Sophie holding Buttons's lead and a bag of dog food – they exchanged glances.

"She really doesn't like Buttons, does she…" Tom muttered. "I'm glad Buttons didn't get left with her. She'd have been down at the dogs' home before she could blink."

"Buttons was only getting out and being naughty because she hadn't been walked, but that wasn't Mr Jenkins's fault," Sophie said loyally.

Sophie's mum was standing at the gate watching for them. "Oh my goodness," she murmured, as she saw everything the boys were carrying. "Look at all that stuff!"

Buttons looked up at her worried face and whimpered. Everyone was cross at the moment, and Mr Jenkins had gone away and left her. She raised her head to the sky and howled.

"You'd better bring her through," Mum said, sighing.

Sophie coaxed Buttons in, and the boys carried all the things into the kitchen, putting them down next to their dad, who looked rather surprised to find a dog eyeing his sandwich enviously.

Dad shook his head, smiling a little. "Looks like you three have got your wish, even if it is only for a week or two. Because that's all it is," he added firmly. "She's going back to Mr Jenkins, so don't get too fond of her, will you?"

It was easy to promise that they wouldn't get too fond of Buttons, but Sophie adored her already and soon she couldn't imagine life without her. Having her to look after every day wasn't boring or hard work, as Dad had warned them. Tom borrowed a DVD on dog-training from the library, and Sophie and the boys started to teach her to walk, heel, sit and stay. They'd always thought of Buttons as rather a naughty dog, because whenever they saw her she'd slipped her lead or tripped someone up. When they'd first taken her for walks, Sophie had held on to her lead so carefully, convinced that Buttons would keep trying to dash off. But although she did pull at her lead a bit, she didn't run away at all. And she was brilliant at the obedience training.

"Labradors are very clever," Dad said, after he'd watched admiringly as they put Buttons through her paces for him. She'd even sat for a whole minute with a dog biscuit between her paws, until Sophie told her she was allowed to eat it.

Buttons was happy, too. She had been very confused that first day, with a new house and a new garden and new people, even if her own basket and her bowls were there. And to start with she had missed Mr Jenkins terribly. Everywhere smelled different and strange, and she followed Sophie around as though she was glued to her.

On Saturday night, Mum had looked at her sad little face and big, round black eyes, and sighed. "I suppose she's going to have to sleep in your room, Sophie. But not on your bed!" she added, as Sophie rushed to hug her.

Although Buttons still thought about Mr Jenkins, she was so happy living with a family who had as much energy as she did. It was the walks that made things so different. An early-morning quick run before breakfast with Sophie. Sometimes a trip down to the shops during the day. And then a proper long walk later on. Up to the common, or along the canal bank. On the Saturday a week after she'd come home with them, the whole family went in the car to a big wood a few miles from the town, and Buttons had a blissful time chasing imaginary rabbits.

That evening when they got home, Sophie sent Rachel an email. She had to type rather slowly, with Buttons sitting on her lap and staring curiously at the computer.

```
To: Rachel
From: Sophie                           📎 Attachment:
Subject: Our new dog?                      Buttons.jpg

Hi Rache!
You'll never guess, we've got a dog!
She's called Buttons, and she's so
cute. I wish you could see her for
real, but I took a photo of her when
we went to the woods today so here it
is. We're only looking after her
while her owner's in hospital, but
she feels like she's actually ours.
```

Sophie stopped typing, and stroked Buttons's soft ears. It was true. Buttons did feel like her dog. "You're the nicest dog I've ever met, do you know that?" she whispered to her, and Buttons turned round and licked her nose lavishly. Sophie giggled, and made *yeeuchh* noises, but really she'd never been happier.

Chapter Six

Sophie had made her mum phone the hospital every day to see how Mr Jenkins was, and to pass on messages about how well Buttons was doing. Mr Jenkins had had to have an operation on his leg, but he was getting better quickly, and the nurses told her that he could have visitors. They even suggested that Sophie, Michael and Tom came, saying that he talked about them all the time and how clever they'd been to rescue him. Mr Jenkins's son had rung the Martins to say how grateful he was to them for looking after Buttons. He begged them to visit too, as he wasn't able to stay away from his family in Scotland for very long, and he was worried that his dad was lonely in the hospital.

So on Monday, just over a week after Mr Jenkins's accident, Sophie and Tom and their mum knocked on the door of Mr Jenkins's room. Luckily it was on the ground floor, as Michael was still outside – with Buttons.

Mr Jenkins was sitting up in bed, reading a newspaper and looking very bored, but he threw it down delightedly when he saw them.

"You came to see me!" he exclaimed. "Is Buttons all right?" he asked eagerly, and Sophie and Tom grinned at each other. Mum had checked with the nurses, and they'd said it was all right to move his bed closer to the window.

"We've got a surprise!" Sophie explained, as she helped to push the bed to the window. "Look!"

Just outside the window was Michael. Except they couldn't really see him, because he was holding Buttons up in front of his face. She wriggled and woofed delightedly as soon as she saw her owner, and tried to lick the glass.

"Oh, I wish we could bring her in," Sophie said sadly. "She's so pleased to see you."

"You've looked after her so well," Mr Jenkins said, smiling. "I can't wait to be out of this place and have her back home with me."

Sophie nodded and smiled, but his words made her feel sick. How could she go back to only seeing Buttons when she walked past Mr Jenkins's garden? She couldn't bear it, after having Buttons almost for her own.

Sophie had known all along that Buttons would have to go home again. But the gorgeous puppy felt like a part of the family now. It was going to be so hard to give her up. She could tell from looking at Mr Jenkins how happy he was to see Buttons. The little dog was all the company he had, now his family had moved away. But Sophie felt like she needed Buttons too. And Buttons needed owners who could give her all the exercise a bouncy young dog had to have. It was so hard.

Sophie was very silent all the way home, and then she took Buttons up to her room (she wasn't supposed to have her on the bed, but Mum pretended not to notice the hairs). Sophie stroked the puppy's velvety ears, and sighed.

Buttons looked at Sophie, her head on one side, her dark eyes sparkling. She gave a hopeful little bark, and nudged her rubber bone towards her. Sometimes they played a really good game where Sophie pretended to pull the bone away, and Buttons pretended to do fierce growling. But maybe Sophie didn't want to play that today.

Sophie tickled her under the chin, and Buttons closed her eyes and whined with pleasure. Sophie knew just where to scratch.

Sophie sniffed back tears. "I can't give you back," she whispered. "I just can't." But she knew she would have to soon.

"Do you really think we can?" Sophie asked excitedly.

Tom nodded. "I think so. She's so good now. We've been training her to walk to heel and stay for nearly a month. Anyway, the common's not too busy today, so hopefully she won't be tempted to dash off and see any other dogs."

"And we've worn her out a good bit already," Michael pointed out.

"OK then." Sophie knelt down next to Buttons, who was sitting, panting happily with her tongue hanging out. It had been a long, hot walk up to the highest point of the common. Sophie's heart started to thump a little as she slipped the catch on Buttons's lead.

How would she react?

Buttons looked round in surprise. Then she gave a pleased little woof, but she didn't make a run for it, as Sophie had dreaded she would. She gazed up at Sophie, as though she was checking Sophie had really meant to let her off the lead. Then she trotted off a few metres, found an enormous stick and dragged it back. She dropped it at Tom's feet, and barked pleadingly at him.

"She wants to play fetch!" Sophie exclaimed. "We haven't even taught her that. I told you she was clever!"

"You couldn't find anything smaller?" Tom pretended to complain, but he flung the stick as far as he could, and Buttons chased after it, barking delightedly.

They played fetch for ages, then walked home, all tired but happy.

Mum was in the kitchen, stirring her coffee round and round, and looking sad.

"What's wrong?" Sophie asked. She had a horrible feeling she already knew.

Mum smiled. "Oh, it's good news, really. Mr Jenkins came home from hospital yesterday. He's much better, and he asked if we could bring Buttons home." She waved a hand at the counter, which was piled up with Buttons's bowls, and the toys Sophie and the boys had bought her. "I've got everything ready. We just need to put it all in her basket."

Sophie slumped into a chair, and Tom and Michael leaned up against the counter, all staring at the sad little pile.

"I can't believe she's going," Michael muttered.

"We just got her to come when she was called. We even let her off the lead today," Tom said flatly.

"I know it's hard, but we always knew she wasn't really our dog..." Mum started. Then she sighed. "No, I can't pretend I won't miss her dreadfully too."

Dad came in from the garden. "You told them then?" he murmured, seeing everyone's miserable faces. "I'm sorry, you lot, but I told Mr Jenkins we'd be round some time this afternoon."

Sophie's eyes filled with tears, as she watched Dad pick up Buttons's basket and start to pack the dog bowls into it.

Dad put the basket down, and came to give Sophie a hug. "You knew it wasn't for always, Sophie. And you'll still be able to see her. I bet Mr Jenkins would love you to visit."

Sophie gulped and nodded, and Buttons nudged her affectionately, licking her hand. She wanted Sophie to cheer up, and come and play in the garden. They could do more of the fetching game, with a ball this time. But Sophie was reaching down to clip her lead back on. Buttons gave her a surprised look. Another walk? Well, that was wonderful, but right now? She was quite tired. She'd been planning to have a good long drink before she did anything else, but her water bowl seemed to have disappeared.

"Come on, Buttons!" Sophie said, trying to sound cheerful. She led the dreary little parade out of the front door.

Buttons's tail started to wag delightedly as they walked up the path to Mr Jenkins's front door.

"See, she's happy to be back," Dad said firmly.

Sophie gulped. She wanted Buttons to be happy, didn't she? It would be horrible if she was upset as well. But all the same … didn't Buttons love them at all? Wouldn't she miss them, too?

Buttons waited for the door to open, her tail swinging back and forth so hard it beat against Sophie's legs. Mr Jenkins's house! Her old house! She was going to see her old owner.

That was what he was now. Her old

owner. She belonged to Sophie these days, and Michael and Tom. But it would still be good to see him.

When the door opened, she tried to fling herself against Mr Jenkins's legs, and lick him all over, but Sophie said, "Down, Buttons! Gently!" and she sat back at once. Of course. She had to be careful with Mr Jenkins. She padded calmly into the hallway, and let Sophie unclip her lead.

"You've done wonders with her," Mr Jenkins said admiringly. "She's so much calmer. She's like a different dog. I just can't thank you enough."

"She's been really good," Sophie said, her voice tight. "And it was fun training her."

Mr Jenkins offered to make them all

tea, but Dad said no, they didn't want to make work for him when he was only just back. Really he wanted to get Sophie and the boys home before Sophie burst into tears.

Buttons watched in surprise as Dad fetched her basket from the hallway and put it down in Mr Jenkins's living room. That was her basket. She would need it. Why were they leaving it here? Then at last she understood, and she whimpered, staring up at Sophie.

"You're home now, Buttons," Sophie said in a very small, shaky voice. She was holding back her tears. "You're going to look after Mr Jenkins, aren't you?" She crouched down to stroke Buttons's nose, and whispered, "Please don't forget us!" in her ear.

Then they left, and Buttons stared after them out of the window. She remembered now that it was her special job to look after her old owner. But she wished she could go home with Sophie.

Chapter Seven

With no Buttons, it felt like there was a hole in the house. She wasn't jumping hopefully round while the Martins got ready to go out, begging with her enormous eyes for them to take her, too. She wasn't there barking with delight when they got home again. She wasn't sitting under the table during meals, her nose wedged lovingly on someone's knee, waiting for crumbs or the odd toast crust. She wasn't on Sophie's bed at night, so Sophie could burrow her toes underneath her warm weight. She was gone.

The summer days stretched out emptily with no dog to walk. Everyone moped around the house, until Mum and Dad sat the children down to talk one morning, just a few days after they'd taken Buttons back.

"Look, I know you all miss Buttons," Dad told them gently. "We had her for nearly a month, long enough for it to feel like she was ours. But try and think of it like this. You did such a good job looking after her, and now she's back where she belongs. Mr Jenkins needs her more than we do – she's all he's got.

We're really proud of you, you know. Especially all that hard work you put into training her." He smiled at their mum, and she nodded. "So we were thinking, maybe it's time we let you have a dog of your own." He sat back and looked at them hopefully, but no one said anything. And then Sophie got up from the table and ran out of the room.

"She only wants Buttons," Michael muttered.

Dad nodded sadly. "I guess it might be a bit too soon. But I mean it, boys. You all did well. And you deserve a dog of your own, when you're ready for one."

That weekend, Dad loaded them all into the car, and refused to tell the children where they were going. "It's a secret," he said, smiling at their mum.

They drove through the town, and Sophie and Michael and Tom tried to work out where they were heading, but Dad wouldn't say if they were right.

Then suddenly Sophie gasped. "The shelter! We're going to the dogs' home, aren't we?" Her voice shook, and she was choking up as she went on. "Please don't, Dad. I don't want to look at other dogs."

"Hey, come on, Sophie, let's just go and see," Tom said excitedly. "Is she right, Dad? Are we going to the shelter?"

"Yup." Dad pulled up close to a big blue sign that said *Rushbrook Animal Shelter*. "And we're here. Come on, everyone."

"Remember we're just looking at the moment," Mum warned the boys, as she walked in with her arm round Sophie, who was trying really hard not to cry.

"We know!" Michael promised, but he and Tom were racing ahead, eager to see all the dogs they were imagining could be theirs.

"I hope this wasn't a bad idea," Mum murmured.

The shelter was full, and all the dogs looked desperate for new homes. Even though Sophie hated the thought of getting another dog – it would feel like she had forgotten Buttons – she had to read the cards over the pens. And once she knew the dogs' names, and their stories, she couldn't help caring about them a little bit.

"Oh, Sophie, look..." Mum was crouching next to the wire front of a pen, gazing at a greyhound, whose long legs were spilling out of his basket. "He's lovely, isn't he? Not that we could get a greyhound, they must need so much exercise. Look at his legs!"

"Actually it says here that older

greyhounds don't like too much exercise. They're quite lazy. He's called Fred and he's looking for a quiet, loving home." Sophie looked at Fred, snoozing happily. "He looks pretty relaxed," she said, giggling.

"Oh, it's nice to see you smile!" Her mum hugged her. "Sophie, you know, even if you don't want a dog now, I'm sure you will one day. You were so wonderful with Buttons."

"That's because she was wonderful," Sophie whispered, digging her nails into her palms so as not to start crying again. "Sorry, Mum." She sniffed hard, and turned back to look at Fred. "He does look lovely, though," she said bravely.

Michael and Tom wanted about six different dogs each, but on the way home in the car even they had to agree that the perfect dog hadn't been at the shelter this time. "But they said they get new dogs all the time, Dad," Tom pointed out. "Can we go back soon?" Sophie leaned against the window and closed her eyes. She wasn't sure she could bear to go again. All those gorgeous dogs, all wanting a home and someone to love them. But Sophie just couldn't love another dog. Not yet.

At Mr Jenkins's house, Buttons was moping, too. She tried not to show it, but it was so hard going back to little short walks. Mr Jenkins was much, much better since his operation, but he still had a stick, and he couldn't walk fast, or for very long. There were no more fantastic runs over the common. No imaginary rabbit-hunting in the woods. Just slow, gentle ambles round the streets. Mr Jenkins couldn't help noticing on their walks that his bouncy, overexcited little puppy had turned into a sad young dog instead. He was glad that she was so well-behaved, of course – Sophie and her brothers had done wonders with her – but he almost wished that just occasionally she would be her silly, happy little self again.

Buttons was very good. She walked to heel, like Tom and Michael and Sophie had shown her. She wondered if Mr Jenkins would let her off the lead, so she could fetch, but she supposed he didn't know she could do that now. She never tried to get out of the garden, even though she could have done, if she'd wanted. She knew how to open the bolt after all. She looked at it sometimes, and wondered about going to see Sophie. But she wasn't supposed to. She didn't belong there any more.

Chapter Eight

Sophie's mum put down the phone, and came slowly back to the table, where everyone was finishing lunch.

"Who was that?" Sophie asked.

"It was Mr Jenkins. He's asked us all round for a cup of tea this afternoon." Mum looked at Sophie, whose face had suddenly crumpled, and Tom and Michael, and said firmly, "I told him of course we would love to. It will be nice to see him."

Sophie stared at her fruit salad, and knew she couldn't eat any more. "Please may I leave the table," she muttered, getting up. She wasn't sure she could be brave enough to go and see Buttons in her real home. Not when she kept imagining her back here.

Her mum sighed and let Sophie go. She looked worriedly at their dad. "It's going to be especially hard for Sophie to see Buttons. She hasn't been in the garden when we've walked past, and I've been grateful. But I suppose it has to happen sooner or later."

Sophie trailed behind the others as they went round to Mr Jenkins's house, walking as slowly as she could. She was desperate to see Buttons, of course she was. And she felt guilty about not going to visit Mr Jenkins sooner.

But she hadn't been able to make herself go. It had been two whole weeks, and she was only just starting to miss Buttons a tiny bit less. If she saw her again, Sophie knew it would be worse than before.

Mr Jenkins answered the door, and there was Buttons, tail wagging furiously, gazing up at Sophie, her big, brown eyes full of love. Sophie had to look away. But she made herself look back and smile. She didn't want Buttons to be miserable too.

Mr Jenkins sent them all to sit down while he made tea and got juice, and then he asked Tom to carry the tray in for him. He seemed a lot better, although he still had his stick. Buttons stayed right next to him the whole time, so when he sat down she sat by him, but she stared at Sophie.

Sophie stared back, sadly.

Buttons edged slightly closer, wriggling on her bottom to where Sophie was sitting next to her mum on the sofa. She wanted to cheer Sophie up. She could try, at least. Inch by inch, she travelled the short distance to the sofa, and leaned her nose lovingly against Sophie's leg.

Sophie stroked her, her eyes filling with tears. "Oh, I've really missed you," she whispered to Buttons. Then she realized that Mr Jenkins was talking, now that he'd made sure everyone had a drink. He sounded very serious.

"I need to ask you all an enormous favour." He looked at Buttons, her head in Sophie's lap, and sighed. "All the time I was in the hospital, I was so keen to be at home, back to normal, with my dog. The same as things were before. But since I've been back home I've realized that what I suspected was right. I wasn't looking after Buttons well enough before. I can't keep up with her!" He smiled sadly. "It's going to be a huge wrench − I've always had a dog, always had big dogs − but I'm going to have to give her up. I couldn't even manage to train her properly!"

He looked at Tom and Michael and Sophie, who were staring back at him wide-eyed. "You three did what I just didn't have the energy to do – turned Buttons into a beautifully behaved dog. Since she's been back with me, she hasn't pulled on her lead, she hasn't barged into me. She's been a treasure. But it isn't fair on her, having to live with a doddery old man. She needs to be able to go racing up to the common. So I've decided. She's going to have to go to the shelter. Unless…"

Sophie gulped.

Mr Jenkins smiled at her. "Unless you can take her. I mean, keep her. Have her as yours. She's missed you, you know. Every time she goes into the garden, she goes and stands by the back fence. She's listening out for you in your garden."

Sophie looked up at her mum, her eyes pleading, and saw that she was laughing.

"We'd told the children they could have their own dog, because they'd looked after Buttons so well. We even went to the shelter to look for one. But none of us could find the dog we wanted, we missed Buttons so much. Of course we'll have her!"

Sophie slipped off the sofa, and hugged Buttons round the neck. "You're coming home with us, Buttons! You're really our dog now!" Then she looked up at Mr Jenkins, frowning. "But what will you do without her? Won't you miss her?"

Mr Jenkins nodded. "Of course I will. But it isn't fair to make her miserable, just to keep me happy."

"I could bring her to see you…" Sophie suggested, and Mr Jenkins smiled gratefully.

They finished their tea, and Mr Jenkins found all Buttons's things for them to take home. He was trying to be cheerful, but Sophie could see he was really upset about giving Buttons away. He was going to be so lonely without her.

Sophie was watching him stroke Buttons lovingly as they said goodbye, when it suddenly came to her.

"Oh! I've just had the most brilliant idea! When we went to the shelter, there was a greyhound, a gorgeous brindled one, called Fred. The card on his pen said he was quite old, and he wanted a quiet, loving home! That's you!"

Mr Jenkins stared at her, frowning thoughtfully as he leaned against the doorframe. "A greyhound … I've never had a greyhound before. I hadn't thought of going to the shelter, but they do want homes for older dogs, don't they…" He smiled. "Do you think you and Buttons would let an old man and an old dog tag along on your walks sometimes, Sophie?"

Buttons looked up at Sophie's glowing face, and Mr Jenkins's smile, and even though she stood beautifully still, her tail waved joyfully. Buttons could see they were happy and she was, too – she was going home.

HOLLY WEBB

Holly Webb started out as a children's book editor, and wrote her first series for the publisher she worked for. She has been writing ever since, with over seventy books to her name. Holly lives in Berkshire, with her husband and three young sons. She has a pet cat called Milly, who is always nosying around when Holly is trying to type on her laptop.

For more information about
Holly Webb visit:

www.holly-webb.com